To Swee

May you love

May it take you far!

Love,

Jacob + Kathryn
Bliss

THE RINGTAILS OF GOODNIGHT ROAD

and the Case of the Stolen Wind-O-Band-Go

Written By Dustin Summers

Illustrated By Katie Mazeika

www.mascotbooks.com

*The Ringtails of Goodnight Road and the Case
of the Stolen Wind-O- Band-Go*

For more information, please contact:
Mascot Books
560 Herndon Parkway #120
Herndon, VA 20170
info@mascotbooks.com

Library of Congress Control Number: 2017905773

CPSIA Code: PBANG0617A
ISBN-13: 978-1-68401-253-4

Printed in the United States

For my mom, who put my first book in my hands.

The author and his mother, August 1984

PROLOGUE

The Ringtail Family lived at the end of Goodnight Road, in the base of a drooping weeping willow that was older than time.

Every morning, the rising sun would shine through the long, thin branches, casting a golden green glow inside the umbrella-like canopy of the tree. Inside and all around the old willow, love filled the warm air of the Ringtail Family's world.

The Ringtail children, Rocky and Wrigley, were students at Forest Elm'enTree, at the end of Cricket Lane. Wrigley was a year older than Rocky, and she enjoyed reminding him of that fact. She was smart and careful and a natural leader. She could also be bossy and unwilling to listen to her younger brother's ideas and suggestions. She enjoyed reading, and it wasn't uncommon to find her curled along a branch in a high-reaching tree, leafing through the pages of an adventure novel or a thrilling crime story. While she would never admit it, Wrigley loved to let her imagination run wild as she pictured herself in the starring role of any story she could get her paws on.

Rocky was fun-loving and happy, content lying on his stomach picking at clover, or reclining on his back looking

for shapes in the stars that hung above the forest night.
He liked to rummage through the trash with his friends
and was often guilty of overeating whenever he could.
While his sister did her best to hide her vivid imagination,
Rocky never felt the need to do so. He loved Halloween,
and even though he wore a mask every day of the year
(like all raccoons), he loved being able to play pretend for
a whole night…plus, he loved all the candy. Rocky would
create elaborate worlds in his mind, complete with exotic
characters and plots; unlike his sister, he wasn't always the
star of the show. Rocky was happy to be part of a larger
group, and sometimes this got him into trouble.

Mom and Pop Ringtail worked as dishwashers at
Chipper's Café, an all-day and (more importantly for the
Ringtail Family) all-night diner that served all the animals
of the forest. They worked over a pair of sinks, where they
took dirty dishes and scrubbed them clean. It was hard
work, but Mom and Pop loved it. The other animals would
sometimes stare in disbelief as Mom and Pop flew through
stacks and stacks of dirty dishes, furiously splashing water
as they washed away food and leftover crumbs. They loved
their two children, and they did their best to make sure
that Rocky and Wrigley had every chance to learn and to
grow and to experience all that the forest had to offer.

Like all raccoons, the family spent their days at night—
preferring to work and play during the evenings and
throughout the twilight and early dawn. Each morning,
as the sky would lighten and the nightbirds would finish
their last songs, the Ringtail Family would pause their
adventures and make their way towards their little home at
the end of Goodnight Road.

And that is where our story begins...

CHAPTER ONE

O ne beautiful early summer morning, Mom, Pop, Rocky and Wrigley were making their way back to Goodnight Road after a long night of work and school. As they walked along the pawpath, the family met friends and neighbors heading towards town on their way to day-work.

"Good morning, Dr. Wilson," Pop said to the portly badger who served as the forest's doctor.

"G'morning, or rather g'night to you and yours, Mr. Ringtail," Dr. Wilson said to Pop as he waddled along, tipping his hat towards the family.

"Where are you off to this morning?" Pop asked.

"I'm heading to Skunk Hollow to deliver Mrs. LaRoma."

"Whoa boy," Pop said, clenching his shoulders and shivering at the thought. "Good luck with all that."

Mom smacked Pop across the arm with a fierce glare. "Please tell her and her entire family that we said, 'Congratulations,'" Mom said to the kindly old doctor.

"Oh, I certainly will," Dr. Wilson said with another tip of his hat as he continued towards town at his slow, plodding pace.

Rocky and Wrigley followed close behind their parents, smiling and nodding to each animal they met. As they passed, Rocky would ask his sister questions.

"What does Tortuga keep under his shell?"

"Why don't we have webbed feet like the Swansons?"

When they passed Portia, the town acupuncturist, Rocky asked, in a low, fast whisper as he always did, "Do you think Portia really shoots those things at patients she doesn't like? My friend, Grover, told me that his cousin's friend's father's next-stump neighbor went to see her, and they got into an argument over the price, and that Portia shot him with fifty quills, and that all porcupines are mean, and that needle therapy is crazy, and that—"

"Rocky," his sister hissed, "don't believe any of that for one second."

"But Grover said—"

"Oh, baloney. If Grover knew half of what he thought he knew, he'd be the class VALE'dictorian."

Rocky shrugged his shoulders and tried not to think too hard about what his sister meant, but his mouth couldn't help but water at the thought of bologna.

Mom and Pop and Rocky and Wrigley were just about to pass their mailbox and part the curtain of branches that surrounded their lovely old tree when there was a feverish flutter of feathers from above.

"Hooli hoo. Hooli hoo. Good morning, Mom and Pop. Good morning, Ringtail family," chirped Maybelle Blue Jay, descending from her lofty perch in her high-rise pent-nest. Maybelle had been the Ringtails' next-tree neighbor for many years; while she meant well, Maybelle had the tendency to put her beak in others' affairs. Her and her bluefeathered friends loved to sit on the branches overlooking the forest and chatter amongst themselves regarding the business of all the animals. She also harbored the slightest crush on Pop Ringtail—a fact that Mom ignored, even when she would frequently show up unannounced and in need of Pop's help to repair something in her ancient, crumbling pent-nest.

"Good morning, Maybelle," Mom called back, looking towards the sky. "How was your evening?"

Maybelle landed in front of the family and set about settling her wings and attempting to smooth her stray feathers. "Oh, it was a lovely evening. Very restful and quite peaceful and serene."

Mom did her best to hide her rolling eyes, but Wrigley caught her and tried to stifle a laugh.

Maybelle lowered her voice and continued, "However, the same cannot be said for poor Felicia."

"The nightingale?" Pop asked.

"Lawds, yes. Lawds, yes. The poor thing. She took a tumble off her roost. Lost eight feathers in the process. Rumor is that she had overdone it on the hummingbird water, if you know what I mean. Um hmm," Maybelle said, with a knowing nod of her bluefeathered head.

"No, Maybelle, we hadn't heard that," Mom added quickly, looking up at her smart aleck husband to make sure he didn't purposely stick his paw in his mouth. "That

is such a shame."

"Yes, yes, you know those nightingales—trying to soar with the eagles, while crawling with—"

"Yes, Maybelle," Mom said, cutting her off, "we know how the old saying goes."

"Anyhoo. I just wanted to make sure you knew. Oh, there goes Old Colonel Cotton slithering through the grass. I wonder if he's heard."

And with that, Maybelle swooped up into the air and sped down the lane.

The Ringtails stared into the sky as she soared away.

"My goodness," Mom said, "she sure loves a good story."

"Or at least half a story," Pop grunted, as he watched Maybelle land in front of Cotton and once again begin her dramatic, animated retelling.

Wrigley looked up at her parents as she knelt to wash an acorn in a puddle of rainwater. "How does Maybelle always know the scoop?" she asked.

"Because she's old and doesn't have anything else to do," Pop said.

Mom elbowed him in the side. "Pop, hush! Maybelle just likes to be in the know, that's all."

Rocky giggled, with a mouthful of berries that he had carried from school. "Wha's thad mean, Pop?" he asked, his teeth working to chew up his snack.

"It means she's a gossip."

Mom hissed at Pop and glared at him with her black masked eyes. "Pop, stop it! Kids, go play a bit before it's time to eat your bedtime gobble. We are having berry casserole and acorn dumplings, and there might even be a dessert or two that Pop and I brought from Chipper's."

"Ohhhh, is it strawberry delight? Is it pumpkin cookies? Is it—"

"Rocky, it will be a surprise, but only if you eat your bedtime gobble first," Mom called to her son as he ran ahead along the willow's pawpath.

"When has that ever been a problem for him?" Wrigley asked wryly, rolling her eyes and following her brother through the willow's sagging branches towards the family's backyard.

"Okay, okay. This time, I am the robber, and I just held up a bank, and you are the crook who was planning to rob the same bank tomorrow morning. Okay, okay? Now you have to chase me. Chase me!"

"Rocky, do we really have to play Crooks and Robbers again? We play this every night," Wrigley sighed as she began to run after her little brother.

But deep down, all young raccoons love to play Crooks and Robbers…even Wrigley Ringtail.

Mom and Pop found a comfortable spot on their favorite log and cuddled close to one another. They sat quietly as they watched their children play and the sun rise over the distant horizon.

CHAPTER TWO

Across the woods at Chipper's Café, the morning crew was preparing for breakfast and another busy day. Sterling, a young squirrel who kept the restaurant's books while he worked towards a counting degree, was adding up the acorns, berries, and smooth pebbles that had been collected during the previous night.

"Wow!" he said as he rechecked his numbers. "Forty nuts and sixty-two berries for a Monday night. That's great!"

Terrence was hopping around the kitchen as he called out orders to his assistant cook, Mockingbird Fred.

"Two carrots over easy."

"Chirp, two carrots over easy."

"One clover medley."

"Chirp, one clover medley."

The young rabbit rarely had a moment to relax as he bounced between the stoves, griddles, and warm ovens. Luckily, Fred was always there to help and to calmly lend a wing.

Claudette, Clementine, and Clarabelle were scurrying about, hustling meals to the hungry diners. As the tables were cleared, the stack of dirty dishes grew in the crowded kitchen sink.

"I feel bad for leaving all of these dishes in the sink for Mom and Pop Ringtail," said Claudette, her nose twitching, her ears wrinkling.

"Don't sweat it, sugar," said Clementine. "They love cleaning those old nasty dishes."

Claudette shrugged her little shoulders and turned quickly to get back to work, but instead ran smack into a sturdy young bear. Claudette's pot of willow bark coffee splashed all over the young cub-uty's freshly pressed uniform.

"Oh, my goodness," Claudette squeaked. "Cub-uty Duncan, I am soooo sorry! Look what I have done."

The young officer smiled warmly at the flustered and embarrassed little mouse.

"It's okay," he said in his deep voice.

"Oh, but it isn't! Look at this mess I've made on your new cub-uty uniform."

"Really, it's okay, Claudette. It's nothing that a little water can't fix."

"I will bring that right over to your table. Here, please, right this way," Claudette said, motioning towards an empty table in the quietest section of the noisy restaurant.

"I take it that Sheriff Samson hasn't arrived yet?" Cub-uty Duncan asked as they walked through the maze of

crowded tables.

"He sure hasn't," Claudette answered, "but as soon as he gets here, I will point him in your direction."

Chipper's was built over the water, and the babbling flow of Jenkins Brook provided a soft soundtrack to the busy morning bustle. Chipper had grown up in a family of beaver builders, and had built the diner many years ago, when his teeth were much sharper and his tail much stronger. He had designed it with high ceilings and sturdy branch walls, so that anyone, from the burliest bear to the teeniest mouse, would feel at home while at his restaurant. Of all the places in the forest, Chipper's was the place to meet, to catch up with friends, and to learn all about the comings and goings within the forest community.

With the scattered schedules of the forest animals, business was always booming, but Chipper never failed to find room and time for all of his customers. He could typically be found in the large round corner booth, drinking a cup of willow bark coffee and talking to his friends and customers. He loved the animals that worked for him, and he marveled at how well they performed their individual jobs.

"G'morning, Mayor," Chipper said as an old gray squirrel made his way through the front door.

"Why, hello there, Chipper," Mayor Hazelton said, smiling brightly through his mouthful of pine nuts. "It sure is a lovely morning,"

"It sure is," Chipper said. "Let me scoot around here, and you can have a seat."

"Oh, that's okay," said the mayor. "I am supposed to be meeting ole Samson and some of his cub-uties in a bit. I'm just a little early."

"You always are," Chipper said, shaking the old squirrel's hand. "Clementine!"

"Yes, Mr. Chipper?" the little mouse asked, wiping her paws on her apron and tucking a pencil behind a large ear as she scurried over to the corner booth.

"Make sure that the mayor has a prime table this morning. He's got a big meeting with the sheriff."

"No, no," Mayor Hazelton said, waving off the request, "don't you go out of your way for us now. We just have a little business to discuss, and we'll be fine with whatever is available. But if it's not too much trouble, I might need a booster seat, just so those big fellas don't accidentally sit on me," he finished with a smile and a wink.

Clementine giggled. "Oh, I think we can handle that. Right this way, Mayor. We've got you a table right by the window."

The old squirrel shook Chipper's paw once again and followed the little mouse to his seat.

Chipper sat back down and took a long drink of his coffee and smiled to himself as he watched all of the animals talk, eat, and laugh with one another.

CHAPTER THREE

As the day was starting at Chipper's, it was ending on Goodnight Road. The Ringtails had cleared the family table, and Mom and Pop were busy scrubbing away the remaining bits of bedtime gobble over the kitchen sink as Rocky and Wrigley got ready for bed. A faint knock echoed from the front door, and each of the Ringtails froze in place with their ears perked and their senses up.

The knock came again, and Wrigley started for the door. "I'll get it," she called. She opened the door to find Grover Gosling, Rocky's best friend and her academic rival, standing on the front porch.

Her eyes narrowed. "Can I help you, Grover?"

"Oh, hi, uh, hi, Wrigley. How are you this evening, I mean this night, I mean morning?" the young goose nervously stammered.

Wrigley kept up her gruff front. "I am fine, Grover. Why are you here?"

"Oh, I had an assignment that I needed to give to Rocky before school," he said, holding up a few sheets of paper.

Wrigley crossed her arms. "I don't know, Grover. It's

getting pretty early. My parents were already asleep. They are going to be so mad."

"Oh, I'm so sorry. I can go. I can just catch up to him later in the evening. I'm sorry. I didn't mean to wake anyone," Grover said, apologizing too many times.

Wrigley looked at him, but shouted over her shoulder. "Rocky! Your friend is here!"

Rocky bounded up behind his sister.

"Hey, Grover!" he said loudly, raising a paw to wave at him even though they were standing directly in front of one another.

"Hey, Rocky. I'm sorry it's so early. I didn't mean to wake your parents."

"Oh, it's okay. They are just cleaning up the dishes."

Grover looked at Wrigley, but she just rolled her eyes.

"I didn't want much. I've been working on our assignment for tomorrow, and I wanted to drop it off for you."

Wrigley smirked. "I finished that assignment hours ago."

The two boys ignored her.

"Okay," Grover said as he turned to leave, "I'll get out of your fur for the morning. See you at school. Have a goodnight, I mean dawn, I mean morning, Wrigley," the awkward little goose stammered.

Wrigley tried not to smile at his helplessness as she closed the door and followed her brother down the hall.

***

The sun shined brightly just beyond their bedroom window, but Rocky and Wrigley lay awake in their beds, unable to sleep. Rocky held a jar of lightning bugs that he had caught earlier in the night, and the pulsing glow was impossible to hide under his sheets. Wrigley could hear him tapping on the glass of the jar and giggling from time to time. She couldn't sleep either. She was restless; as was often the case, once something was on her mind, it was difficult to let go of it until she took action.

"Rocky," she whispered.

No response.

"ROCKY," she said louder, but in an urgent whisper.

Her brother popped his head and paws from under the covers. "What?"

She got right to the point. "I've been thinking about what Pop said earlier."

"About the desserts? Me too. I know we had the strawberry delight earlier, buuuuuuuut I was thinking that they might have been holding out on us. Do you think they had more and just hid them from us? Want to go look for them?"

"No, Rocky, I was not thinking about the desserts," she said with a sigh. "I was thinking about Maybelle, about how she's old and only gets half of the story right. Remember?"

Rocky nodded his head.

"So I was thinking…why don't we start a newspaper?"

"Huh?"

Wrigley sat up in her bed and switched on the Twi'Lite that was plugged in beside her bed giving the room a faint soft glow. "I think we should start a newspaper for the forest. Look, I've got it all worked out. We can do our reporting after school, write up our articles, and get the news out to everyone on their way to work in the morning."

"When did you come up with all of this?"

"I was thinking about it while we were playing in the backyard."

"During Crooks and Robbers?"

"Yeah. I was thinking about what would happen if there really was a crime in the forest. How would everyone get the facts? How would they know what was going on?"

Rocky thought for a second. "Doesn't Sheriff Samson typically take care of all of that?" he asked, the glow from the jar lighting the confused look on his face.

"Oh, yeah. Of course. Samson handles all of that, but I'm just thinking that it would be nice for the other animals to have an accurate account of the news and all of the events going on in the woods."

"Hmmm." Rocky thought for a bit. He shook the jar of fireflies and finally said, "You know, I think that's a great idea."

"Great! And we could also cover other events like

birthday parties, some sports, and maybe we can even do a little investigative reporting," Wrigley said, still whispering across the room to her brother.

Rocky looked up from his glowing jar. "Why do we need to wear vests when we are doing our reporting? Is that what newspaper people do?"

It took Wrigley a second to realize where the breakdown in communication had occurred. She closed her eyes and took a deep breath. "No, Rocky. 'In-vest-i-ga-tive,' not 'in vests.' I just mean that we may have to dig deep into a story to find the truth."

"Oh, okay," Rocky said, "but raccoons really don't dig that much. We typically just find food on the forest floor. I don't know how good we'll be at digging deep."

"Goodnight, Rocky," she said with a sigh.

"Goodnight, sis," he said as he pulled the covers back over his head and stared deeply into his jar of dancing fireflies.

CHAPTER FOUR

The next night, on the way home from elm'entree school, the Ringtail children set to work. As usual, Wrigley had a plan.

"We need to talk to as many animals as we can. Pop says that Maybelle only gets half the story, and I don't want to make that mistake. What do you think about talking to the Ribbits first?"

"I like it," Rocky said. "They live on the land and in the water, so they probably know what's going on all over the forest."

"Right, I was thinking the same thing. We also need to talk to some day animals, as well as other night animals like us."

"I agree. We also need a good name for our newspaper," Rocky said as he kicked at a little pebble along the side of the path.

"That can wait," Wrigley said sharply. "We need good stories first."

"How about *Midnight Express*?" said Rocky, ignoring his sister's criticism.

"No, Rocky. That sounds like a terrifying train."

"Hmm. Okay. How about *The Sunrise Sampler*? You know, because everyone will be reading it in the morning."

Wrigley stopped and looked at her brother. "Rocky, the sunrise sampler is a breakfast dish at the diner."

"Oh, that's right. I knew it sounded familiar."

"We can talk about this later. Grab your notepad out of your rac-pack, and let's get to work. We don't have much time before we have to get back home." Rocky dug through his loose papers and gnawed pencils until he found his ringed notebook hiding at the bottom of his rac-pack.

With a fresh notebook, four sharpened pencils, and only a couple of hours in which to work, Rocky and Wrigley set out to find some news.

They walked first to Puddle Pond, where the Ribbit Family lived in a cluster of pale green lily pads.

"Hey Rocky and Wrigley," Dale Ribbit croaked as they made their way along the muddy shore. "If you're looking for Huckleberry, he isn't home from school yet. I think he has jumping practice this morning."

"That's okay," Wrigley called back, sliding slightly as she looked for firm footing in the soft mud. "We were actually just hoping to talk to anyone in your family."

"Oh, really?" Dale said, "Is something wrong?"

"Oh, not at all," she said. "Rocky and I are actually starting a newspaper for the forest, and we were hoping that maybe you could point us towards some stories."

"I see," Dale said as he flung his tongue towards a buzzing fly. THRWEERP. "I think that's a fantastic idea. The forest definitely needs a paper."

"Yeah, and we are going to call it *The Sunrise Sampler*," Rocky said, dramatically stamping out the words of the title in the air with his front paws.

Wrigley turned sharply. "We are not calling it *The Sunrise Sampler*," she hissed through her clenched teeth.

Dale croak-kled, the way all bullfrogs laugh, and said, "I'm sorry, kids. I'm afraid that I don't have any hot news. You know me, I'm on dis-animality these days, ever since my old leg gave out. I don't leave the lily pad too often anymore. It's hard for an old bullfrog who can no longer jump. There isn't a day that goes by that I don't wish I hadn't jumped onto that slippery rock. I told my boss that it was slick with slime, but 'Ohhhh, never mind that,' he said, 'you've got to get over there and clear out those flies,' he said. And wouldn't you know it, ole Dale missed his landing and sprawled all over creation. I've been laid up with this old busted leg ever since, just laying around the lily pad and waiting on my dis-animality checks, which are usually late, by the way."

Rocky and Wrigley awkwardly cut their eyes towards one another. They hadn't expected such a long account of Dale's grievances.

"We are awfully sad to hear about that, Mr. Ribbit," Wrigley offered, "and we are sorry that you don't have any news leads for us either."

"Yeah, kids, me too. It's just a sad state of affairs all around these days." Then, his eyes lit up for the briefest of seconds. "But you could—" He stopped short as he second-guessed himself. "No. Never mind, that's probably not the best idea."

"No, no, what is it?" Wrigley asked, her ears perking up and her eyes widening.

"I was going to say that you could check with Chirp and the Hoot Owls."

"The rock band?" Rocky asked excitedly.

"Yep. They are playing over at the Strut Shack, but I don't think you kids should go down there. If I happen to see Chirp or one of the Hoots, I'll tell them you are looking for some scoops, and maybe you can meet them down at Chipper's."

Wrigley thought it over. "Sure, Mr. Ribbit. That sounds good to us."

"Sorry that I wasn't more help."

"That's okay," she said. "Tell Huckleberry we said 'Hi.'"

"I sure will—and kids," he called as they turned to leave, "stay away from slimy and slick rocks."

Wrigley motioned for Rocky to follow her, and the kids made their way up the bank.

"So, now where are we going?"

Wrigley turned to her brother. "I'll tell you where," she said, with a gleam in her large black eyes. "We're going to the Strut Shack."

CHAPTER FIVE

The Witching Hour Dance Hall and Strut Shack sat on the edge of the FarAway Woods, near the border of the forest and the neighboring barnyard, where all sorts of animals would come to dance and strut and squawk and crow. The Ringtails had never been there, but they knew where it was and had heard rumors about it from their older forest friends.

Rocky and Wrigley made their way through the tall trees just as the morning light began to peek through the overhead leaves.

"There it is," Rocky gasped. The blinking green and pink sign was missing a letter or two—the result of a particular cardinal's long night several months ago.

"Rocky, we have to be careful and quiet. We could get in trouble for sneaking over here."

"No problem. We'll just pretend like we're playing Crooks and Robbers. They always have to be quiet when they are sneaking into a bank."

Wrigley rolled her eyes.

The kids made their way down the hill, careful to stay low

in the remaining shadows stretching across the forest floor. Once at the back window, Rocky climbed up and peered over the edge to look inside. It was just as he had imagined it—pigs and chickens, birds and squirrels, all dancing and having a great time. The air was thick with dust and the occasional clump of loose hay falling from the overhead loft or thrown by a rowdy patron. On stage, Chirp and the Hoot Owls were finishing a late night set of songs.

"Chirp and his band are about to pack up their stuff," Rocky called down to his sister, his arms straining to hold himself up.

Wrigley looked around the dirt lot surrounding the Strut Shack, but did not spy the band's kooky Wind-O-Band-Go with 'Chirp and the Hoot Owls' scrawled across the side in red chicken scratch script. Rocky and Wrigley had seen the band fly to and from gigs in this contraption several times. Each member of the Owls would hold a strap attached to one side of the large nest, and Chirp would sit atop their gear, playing his harmonica and singing as his bandmates flapped along towards wherever they were playing. It looked like a great way to get to and from shows, and the unusual sight of the owls transporting a loud, chirping, singing, clamoring cricket in such a strange contraption was a great way to generate buzz for an upcoming gig.

"Rocky, get down so we can wait for them in the parking lot," Wrigley said to her brother, tugging on his tail.

Rocky's legs kicked against the shack's wall as he strained to catch one more look inside the nightclub before he tumbled to the dirt.

It didn't take long for Chirp and his bandmates to emerge from the noisy air of the Strut Shack. Rocky and Wrigley held back in the shadows until the band had moved all of their gear outside into a large pile, where they huddled together and relaxed after a long night of music.

As frequent guests of Chipper's Café, Rocky and Wrigley had seen the band many times over the years, but Rocky was always a little too excited to talk to them.

"Hey, Chirp!" Rocky bellowed from the dark.

Chirp jumped and skittered his legs together. "Oh, Rocky, hey, man. You scared me, man. What's up?"

"I'm sorry, Chirp. My sis and I are just, you know, chillin' and hangin' tonight. Wha's up with you, man?" Rocky said, trying to sound the way he imagined musicians talked to one another.

Wrigley looked at him as if he had lost his mind. "Chirp, what my brother really means is we are actually working on a newspaper, and we were hoping that you might have a scoop or two for us."

"Oh, that's great," piped up Moonie, the drummer. "Who who who are you going to write about?"

"We don't know yet," said Wrigley. "We were thinking that you guys might have some good ideas."

Chirp scratched his head with his hind leg as he thought. "I'm stumped. What about you guys?" he asked, turning towards his bandmates.

'Squito, the bassist, shrugged. Moonie just shook his head in a long side-to-side swivel.

"Sorry, little dude and dudette. It looks like you're out of

luck," Chirp said.

Rocky and Wrigley dropped their heads. After two stops, they were striking out on their plan to find and report the forest's news.

"That's okay, guys," Rocky said. "We appreciate you putting your heads together for us. Hey, and maybe we can come catch your groovy tunes sometime."

Wrigley rolled her eyes again, and the Ringtail children turned to head towards Goodnight Road.

It was then that Angus, the lead guitar player, spoke up and said, "Maybe you can find out who who who swiped our Wind-O-Band-Go."

Rocky and Wrigley stopped in their tracks and turned towards the band.

Chirp slapped his forehead. "Oh yeah, duh, man," he laughed to himself. "The Wind-O-Band-Go. Oops. Yeah, someone swiped our traveling nest the other night. I suppose that's a story."

It was a story—one that Rocky and Wrigley intended to write.

CHAPTER SIX

Rocky and Wrigley could barely sit still the following night in their elm'entree school classes. They wiggled in their seats and waited impatiently for the final bell, so that they could get to work on their reporting for the first edition of the newspaper.

Even though they had a great lead for their first cover story, they had successfully managed to get information for a few other stories from their classmates.

Priscilla, the beautiful, flighty swan, had won the forest beauty pageant the previous weekend. Grover's older brother, Gregory, was getting married next month. And Huckleberry Ribbit had qualified for several jumping events at the upcoming HopLympics.

As they turned off Cricket Lane and onto Truffle Street, heading towards downwoods, the raccoon children reviewed the details that Angus, Moonie, 'Squito, and Chirp had given them the previous night.

"Okay," Wrigley began, flipping through the pages of her ringed notebook, "here's what we know. The Wind-O-Band-Go disappeared three nights ago. It was parked at Chirp's den on Turkey Run Road. It's typically transported by three full-grown owls, so it's neither little nor easily moved."

Rocky nodded along as his sister recounted the facts.

"We also have this picture that we can run with the story," Wrigley said as she flapped the photograph that Chirp had given her the previous night. In it, the Hoot Owls were flying low over the forest floor, carrying the Wind-O-Band-Go as Chirp sat atop a mountain of musical equipment—amplifiers, cables and cords, instruments, trunks and cases, microphones, and, of course, an ample number of speakers. There was little doubt that Chirp and the Hoot Owls was the loudest band in the forest. Between their thunderous volume and the rambling Wind-O-Band-Go, they created a stir wherever they went.

"Our suspect list is pretty short at the moment. According to 'Squito, Jimi Jay, the band's former guitarist, had tried to buy the Wind-O-Band-Go several weeks ago, but he was playing at the Barn Yard Harvest Moon Festival the night it went missing," Wrigley continued. "Of course, Rasso is always a suspect when these sorts of things happen, but otherwise, I'm stumped."

Rasso was a shady rat who typically caught the blame for all that went wrong in the forest. He had worked at Chipper's for a bit, but a rat in the kitchen made the customers uncomfortable. Next, he went to work for LaRoma Brothers Sanitation, the forest's garbage removal service, but he was caught several times nosing through the animals' trash and swiping items that he thought he could use around his nest. It was this habit that made Wrigley think that he might, once again, be at the root of this crime.

Rocky scratched behind his ear and groaned in frustration. "What do you think we should do?" he asked his sister.

"I don't really know, but since Rasso is our only suspect, maybe we should stakeout the road to his den."

Rocky jumped. "But that's Tumblecreek Road! That place is terrifying. I don't want to go down there. There are briars and thorns and it's really dark, even for raccoons, and Grover said that he—"

"Relax," she said. "We don't even have to go down there at all. All of the traffic off Tumblecreek Road runs right behind Chipper's Café. I say we go down there and watch for any suspicious activity."

"But Rasso isn't actually a suspect. We're just blaming him because we don't know who else would do this."

"Rocky, stop making excuses. Isn't Rasso usually tied up in situations like this?"

Rocky twiddled his paws, but he couldn't think of a time when Rasso hadn't been to blame. "What are we going to do if Mom and Pop see us?"

"They won't," Wrigley said with confidence. "We are going to hide under the dumpster and out of sight of all of the customers…and employees."

It was enough to calm his fears. Rocky loved dumpsters, and while his sister was plotting this secret surveillance mission, his mouth was already watering with the thought of all of those tasty trash treats.

CHAPTER SEVEN

Rocky and Wrigley hid low under the dumpster at Chipper's Café, peering out into the fading night.

Rocky sniffed the air. "Something smells delicious. What is that? Old apples?" He wrinkled his nose as he concentrated. "No, no! It's day-old cabbage! Oh, my favorite!"

"Would you knock it off?" his sister scolded. "We are investigative journalists, and that means we have to be quiet."

"Oh, yeah. That's right. I'm sorry." Rocky lowered his head so that he could better see from beneath the dumpster as he did his best to ignore his watering mouth.

Wrigley scanned the night, but even with her great eyesight, she didn't spy anything out of the ordinary.

"So, Wrigley," Rocky began in a soft whisper, so as not to unnerve his sister, "I was thinking, since we have a few minutes tonight, maybe we could finally settle on a name for our paper."

Wrigley played along. "Okay, Rocky. Dare I ask what you want to go with?"

La Roma Brothers Sanitation
Tumblecreek Road
Puddle Pond
Gruffman's Marsh
Elm'enTree
CrossTrails

Rocky pulled a crumpled piece of paper out of his rac-pack. "Okay," he began, "tell me what you think of these: *The Nightly News*?"

"Boring."

"*The Evening Edition?*"

"More boring."

"*Night Eyes?*"

"Creepy."

"*While You Were Sleeping?*"

"Hmmm. That's clever. I don't hate it."

"Okay," Rocky said, "I will go ahead and circle that one, and—"

"Shh!!!" Wrigley hissed.

At the edge of the clearing, something was moving.

"Rocky, be still!!!"

"I'm not mov—"

She cut him off again.

Wrigley and Rocky squinted their eyes and tensed their tails under them as they strained to make out who or what was walking their way.

It was something big, moving slowly, shuffling across the loose dirt of the clearing.

"What is that?" Rocky asked.

"I don't know, but whatever it is, it won't see us if we stay still and quiet," Wrigley said as she turned to glare at her brother.

Rocky ducked his head but mocked her as he returned to look towards the end of the clearing. As whatever it was neared them, Wrigley and Rocky could make out voices.

"Pick up your side."

"I'm trying," replied a strained voice.

"Try harder."

More shuffling, more straining.

The moonless night did little to provide help as Rocky and Wrigley looked towards the distance. They could make out two figures struggling to haul something large and cumbersome.

"That's the Wind-O-Band-Go, Rocky! We caught them!" she said, trying her best to not let excitement overcome her whisper.

"You're right. That's the Wind-O-Band-Go, buuuuuuuut… who are the critters carrying it?" Rocky said, using every bit of his keen raccoon eyesight to make out the features and details of the culprits.

"Is that Rasso?" Wrigley asked. She perked up her ears, hoping she'd be able to pick up voices, but the thieves were still too far in the distance. "Who is that? It has to be Rasso, right? Who could be with him?" she frantically whispered.

The shadowy figures passed into the deeper shadows and their voices faded over the path. Rocky and Wrigley sat stunned, recounting what they had just witnessed.

After enough silence had passed, Rocky spoke first. "What in the world did we just see?"

For once, his sister didn't tell him to hush.

CHAPTER EIGHT

Rocky and Wrigley hurried down the road, chattering to one another as they ran.

"I can't believe it. I just can't believe it," Wrigley said, panting, as her rac-pack bobbed back and forth with each stride.

"I know! What are the odds that we'd catch the thief red-pawed'ed?" Rocky called as he struggled to keep up with her. "Wrigley, please, wait up."

Wrigley stopped under a pine tree as her little brother doubled over, panting and struggling to catch his breath.

"It's the scoop that we've been needing, and to think we caught him in the act of actually moving the stolen Wind-O-Band-Go," she said.

Rocky plopped into the soft bed of pine needles, his belly rising and falling as he tried to slow his breathing. He looked up at his sister and wrinkled his face. "But what did we see? I sure couldn't tell who it was."

Wrigley caught her breath. "It was obviously Rasso and an accomplice, right?"

"Was it?" Rocky asked, "I couldn't tell. It was too dark."

"I mean, it would have to be. Whoever we saw was coming from the direction of Rasso's den. And isn't Rasso typically the culprit in things like this?"

Rocky scratched his head as he tried to collect his thoughts.

"Come on," she said. "We have to get this down right now, while the details are still fresh. That means we are going to have to work all morning while Mom and Pop are sleeping."

"Stay up all morning? Won't we get in trouble?" Rocky asked.

His sister glanced over her shoulder, and with a mischievous look in her eye, smiled at him. "Not if we don't get caught."

Rocky started to say something but instead slowly began to run after his sister as they continued towards home.

The kids made their way into the canopy of the willow tree just as Mom was walking onto the front steps.

"Where have you been?" she said, her paws balled into knots and firmly planted on her hips.

"We're sorry, Mom," Wrigley said. "We were playing and just let time get away from us."

"Yeah, Mom," Rocky said, pulling his rac-pack off and dropping it on the steps, "we got busy, and then, poof, bang, all of a sudden it was morning. I don't know. It was the craziest thing ever." He was sweating profusely with his front paws on his knees, gasping for breath.

Mom looked at her two raccoon kids and knew she wasn't getting the full story, but they looked fine and unharmed, even if they were a little dirty and smelled a bit like garbage.

"Okay, you two need to get inside and take your baths before you sit down at my table."

"But Moooooooooom," Rocky began to whine.

"No debate, Rocky. You and your sister stink, and you've had Pop and me worried to death."

Wrigley took her brother by the elbow and began to lead him inside. "She's right, Rocky. We probably do need to get cleaned up." Once they were inside and out of earshot of their mother, Wrigley added, "Plus, as soon as we get this over with, we can get started on our first issue."

Mom stood in the door and watched her two children disappear around the corner of the willow's hallway. She knew they were up to something, but couldn't quite put her paw on it. She walked into the family room, where Pop was dozing in the Laz-E-Log.

"Your children are home," she said as she flopped onto the couch beside his favorite chair.

"Everyone in one piece?" he asked, his eyes still closed, his paws still folded over his belly.

"Yeah, they just stink."

Pop chuckled. "I ran into Dale Ribbit earlier tonight. He said the kids stopped by his pad last night for 'stories of the forest.' Whatever that means." Even without opening his eyes, Pop knew that Mom would be confused. "Apparently they are working on a newspaper or some such," he continued.

Mom thought this over. "Hmm," she said, "this could be interesting."

"Um hmm," Pop said.

Mom sat quietly and stewed on her own thoughts as Pop tried once again to drift off to a deeper sleep, one he hoped would be filled with dreams of soft pumpkin seeds and pools of clear spring rain. However, there was a knock at the door, and Pop groaned as he pulled himself up out of his chair and started down the hall.

"I'll get it," he grumpily said. He could hear her calling from the front porch before he was even able to open the door.

"Hooli hoo. Hooli hoo."

Pop opened the door to find Maybelle Blue Jay standing there, smiling and wearing her best jewelry.

"Oh, Pop," Maybelle began, "could you help an old bird out?"

"What seems to be the trouble, Maybelle?"

"I'm just having the hardest time with my old nest. I declare, it's falling in around me."

"Oh, we can't have that," Pop said, resigning himself to the fact that his nap would have to wait.

"Would you mind coming over to make just a couple of

quick repairs? I'd like to clean up the roost around my nest. If I am relegated to living out my final years in that decrepit old shack, I may as well have a lovely perching area from which to enjoy the evening air."

Pop groaned as he thought about the climb he was about to make to the top of Maybelle's tree. What a waste of time, he thought, hardly anyone can see her old nest from the forest floor anyway. She's just trying to keep up appearances for her old bluefeathered friends.

"Give me just a second to grab a few tools, Miss Maybelle," Pop said as he turned to walk towards the little cubby where he stored his tools.

Maybelle watched him gather his things. "Oh, there's no rush. I've got all the time in the world."

"Hmpf. I bet you do," Pop said under his breath.

CHAPTER NINE

Later that evening, behind the evening shades of Rocky and Wrigley's room, as their parents slept down the hall, the two Ringtail children were busy at work.

Throughout the day, Rocky would write and Wrigley would make corrections. Then they'd switch tasks, each making notes and scribbles along the edge of each page. They'd rewrite and edit until they were satisfied that each article was perfectly perfect.

Slowly, the newspaper began to take shape. With a severe case of writer's block and out of fear of his further suggestions, Wrigley relented on the paper's name. *While You Were Sleeping* wasn't an awful name, and she supposed that it would suffice. She was more concerned with the content and quality of their stories, and she did her best to accurately relay the details and to keep Rocky on track throughout the long hours. The kids had covered the schedule for upcoming Forest Council meetings, local birth announcements, wedding announcements, sports, and most importantly, the theft of Chirp and the Hoot Owls' Wind-O-Band-Go.

While the writing took focus and creativity, the hardest part was the copying and the copying…and the copying.

After hours of rewriting and repeating, Rocky groaned, "How many of these do we have to make?"

Wrigley rubbed her tired eyes and looked over at her exhausted little brother. "We can probably stop for now. Let's get some sleep. It's almost sunset anyway. We'll get through school, make a few more copies, and then we can get them out by next sunrise. Mom and Pop will be up in a just a little bit anyway."

"Sounds good to me," Rocky said with a big yawn, as he put a cap on his ink pen and collapsed into his soft raccoon bed.

He was asleep before Wrigley could even switch off their Twi'Lite.

CHAPTER TEN

O nce again, elm'entree school was difficult for Rocky
and Wrigley that night. While they were excited for
their newspaper to finally be ready, they were exhausted
from their long day of writing and copying. At lunch,
Rocky could barely eat, which was very unusual for him.
Instead, he found a quiet spot and curled up to steal a
quick midnight nap.

Wrigley was anxious too. She was worried about how
others would react to the paper, whether it was written
perfectly, whether she could have done more to make it a
success. She spent the day fidgeting in her seat, twirling her
pencil in her hair, and nibbling at her claws.

After school, the kids went straight home and ate a fast
bedtime gobble with their parents. Then they went to their
room and put the finishing touches on the paper.

Finally, Wrigley declared that they were done. "Finished,"
she said, throwing her arms in the air and high-pawing her
brother.

"Thank heavens. I'm going blind from making so many
copies," he said, crossing his eyes and making a silly face.

Wrigley laughed. "Alright," she said, "let's pack 'em up and get ready to make some deliveries."

She and Rocky bundled the issues together and stuffed them into their rac-packs. The two little raccoons then waddled into the family's nightroom, weighed down by their heavy loads.

"Mom! Pop!" Wrigley called, "Rocky and I have to go drop something off at Grover's."

"Yeah, yeah," Rocky said, nervously coming up with a story, "he needs to, uh, see some counting work that Wrigley did earlier tonight. Uh yeah, it shouldn't take long."

Mom tried not to smile as she looked at her children, who were obviously carrying their weight in newspapers in their small rac-packs.

"Okay," she said, "don't stay out too early…"

But her voice trailed away as her two slow moving children ran as quickly as they could out the front door and down the pawpath towards town.

Rocky and Wrigley worked quickly, and with each delivery, their packs got lighter and they moved a little faster. They stopped at Puddle Pond, at the CrossTrails, slipped over to the Strut Shack, and finally dropped a bundle at Chipper's.

"That's it," Rocky said, wiping his paws and zipping up his empty rac-pack.

"I think we did a great job," Wrigley said.

"I do too. But maybe next time, we find someone to help out with all of the silly copying."

Wrigley smiled. "Yeah, that was terrible. But Rocky, you did a great job. Thank you for all of your help."

"You did a great job, too, sis. I couldn't have come up with all of those stories without you."

Rocky gave his sister a big raccoon hug. Even though she was surprised, Wrigley appreciated it. They had worked hard over the past few nights. After a few seconds, she said with a little laugh, "Okay, Rocky, enough of that. Let's go home."

The Ringtail children turned towards Goodnight Road and began the walk towards the old willow tree. It was still mostly dark as Rocky and Wrigley made their way home, and the cool forest air hung heavy and still. But soon, the sun would rise, and with it, a whole new story would begin.

INTERLUDE

Some forest mornings arrive with rain, with sprinkles and showers and drops and drips bouncing off the lively green leaves of outstretched trees. The water travels down limbs and trunks, leaving behind slick black bark in its wake before settling into pools along the forest floor. It hangs in the dense wooded air and breathes life into the plants and animals of the world.

Perhaps if it had merely rained on the morning that Rocky and Wrigley's paper was published, what happened next could have been avoided. The papers would have turned into a mangled mush of smeared words, and while the Ringtail children would have been disappointed and a few wrongdoers might have escaped, everyone would have been spared what was to come.

It wasn't that the paper was poorly written or poorly constructed—quite the contrary. The newspaper's masthead was clean and professional:

While You Were Sleeping

Vol. 1, Issue 1

And it wasn't that the stories were of little interest to the forest readers:

Huckleberry Ribbit to Compete in HopLympics

Forest Jumping Champion Huckleberry Ribbit has qualified for the HopLympics and will be representing our community in the upcoming event. Huckleberry is a two-time Forest champion, and this will be his first trip to the HopLympics after qualifying at the recent InterForest Trail Trials.

"Im'a excited 'bout headin' to that there jumpin' contest," Huck said earlier this week. "There'll be plenta ole good jumpers there, but I'm a-lookin' forward to thumpin' 'em all."

Huck's parents, Dale and Frida, will be joining him at the HopLympics, and a support fund has been established at First Forest Stash and Bury, to assist with the family's travel expenses.

Or...

Swanson to Marry Gosling in Five Ring Ceremony

Michael and Kathleen Swanson of Jenkins Brook are pleased to announce the upcoming marriage of their daughter, Stacy, to Gregory Gosling, son of Maverick and Charlotte Gosling of Woodlawn Stream.

Stacy, one of the family's seven swimmers, is employed at the Puddle Pond Pollywog Nursery and Daycare.

Gregory, the oldest of six Gosling children, serves as a nesting market analyst at Golden Egg Stash and Bury.

Serving as the groom's best man will be Gosling's childhood friend and local drag racer Toddy Turtle, while the bride's uptree neighbor, Deborah Dove, will fill the maid of honor role. The ceremony will take place at the Parsonage of the Pear Tree, and will be presided over by Reverend Cocotte.

A reception will follow at Milk Maid's Tavern, with entertainment provided by local bands the Leapin' Loons and the Piping Piners, which feature a total of twelve female drummers, nine of whom also dance.

The couple plans to settle in a newly purchased nest in The Cove at Puddle Pond near the bride's place of employment.

All in-woods animals are invited to attend, and the families are calling all birds to help deliver the announcements to out-of-forest guests.

…but for all of the stories and reports, it was, of course, the front page feature that garnered the most attention.

Splashed in huge, bold letters just under the paper's masthead, was the headline:

Theft in the Forest Community

Breaking News!

…and it was there that Rocky and Wrigley ran their story…

Somewhere amongst us, in our fair forest community, lurks a cold-blooded thief. In the dead of night, when the day animals sleep and the night animals are hard at work, a criminal or team of criminals lurks in the shadows, intent on doing harm.

It was a sensational lede, and it caught the attention of each forest reader. In the story that followed, Rocky and Wrigley laid out what they knew, what they assumed, and what they had outright guessed.

Less than a week ago, our beloved forest troubadours, Chirp and the Hoot Owls, had their prized Wind-O-Band-Go stolen by a nefarious thief. Following a long night's work, the band slept in their house on Turkey Run Road. Yet outside, under the cover of darkness, the Wind-O-Band-Go was targeted, swiped, and ferreted away. Many of us have seen the Wind-O-Band-Go soaring overhead, carrying the band to performances or meandering through the trees as they made their way home in the early mornings.

Yet someone has seen fit to swipe this useful transport vehicle and claim it as their own. Upon interviewing Chirp and the Hoot Owls a mere three nights ago and learning of this misdeed, your intrepid reporters saw fit to investigate this matter directly.

Stowing away under a snug dumpster, we observed a criminal duo transporting the stolen Wind-O-Band-Go along Tumblecreek Road, away from Gruffman's Marsh; from our vantage point, however, we were unable to discern who or what the miscreants were. Given the proximity of the purloined item to the home of our community's most notorious criminal, it is certain that Rasso the Rat is one of the perpetrators. However, as reported here first, he did not act alone. While we did our best to discern the identity of the accomplice, we were unable to do so.

We implore you, as upstanding citizens of the forest community, to do your part in apprehending these evildoers.

To report any and all anonymous tips, please contact Sheriff Samson at the downwoods precinct.

The story, like each story in the paper, had been the work of both raccoons—both had worked hard to craft the article and to write something that others would want to read. The excitable first sentence was Wrigley's favorite part.

"See if this grabs your attention," she'd asked Rocky before reading it to him the first time.

Rocky's eye mask wrinkled. "But if we say, 'cold-blooded,' that eliminates all of the 'warm-blooded' animals, like us

and like Rasso."

"Hmmm." Wrigley had to take a moment to reason through her thoughts. "Good point, but that's how all of the criminals in the books I read are described."

Rocky had read and reread the story. Something about it bothered him. He didn't know if it was because he couldn't understand some of the words or if it was the way the story seemed to point a paw for the reader. Whatever it was, it had made him uneasy, but he could see the obvious pride that his sister took in the finished product. He could see how her eyes widened as she read over the words they had written. So, instead of raising an objection, he had simply let it go.

It had been an exhausting night's work, and now, as their first readers opened the paper, Rocky and Wrigley were tucked into their beds, sleeping soundly.

CHAPTER ELEVEN

Across town, Virgil Hoppers was out for his morning run. Unlike his brother Terrence, who was typically busy with his cook duties at Chipper's or with his numerous children, Virgil made certain that he found time to exercise regularly. He enjoyed the stillness of the early mornings, and his long runs along the forest trails helped to start his day on the right foot.

Having made several laps around town, Virgil was exhausted, and so he stopped to rest at the CrossTrails intersection. Under a large oak tree set alongside the trail, he spied the bundle of newspapers that Rocky and Wrigley had delivered earlier in the dawn. Virgil picked up the top copy and began to read. The muscular rabbit was out of breath from his workout, and salty sweat dripped down his hare hair and into his eyes.

"Uhhh, this is going to be bad," he said to himself as he looked over the cover story.

He re-read the accusations, and he couldn't help himself from drawing conclusions, thinking about who could be responsible. Soon, the morning would begin for the daytime animals, and Virgil knew that everyone in the community would want to get their paws on this inaugural issue of *While You Were Sleeping.*

He tucked his copy under his arm and hurriedly hopped down the lane.

***

Later that morning at Chipper's Café, the customers were huddled low over their tables, abuzz as they discussed the morning paper. Claudette, Clementine, and Clarabelle caught snippets of conversations as they circled the dining room, refilling glasses of willow bark coffee and rainwater tea.

"…saw Terrence looking mighty exhausted and suspicious…"

"…know he has babies on the way. I bet he could use a fancy Wind-O-Band-Go…"

"…Ringtail kids sure stirred up some trouble this time…"

"…don't know if we want them spyin' around…"

"…yeah, but they did a good job…"

"…I'd read it again…"

"…nah, those kids are troublemakers…"

"…Rasso is obviously behind this…"

"…um hmm, guaranteed…"

"My goodness," said Clementine, as she waited on a clover medley to appear from the kitchen, "everyone seems to be suspicious of everyone."

Clarabelle added a few elm leaves to a pitcher of tea. "I

know," she said, "everyone is an investigator this morning."

"How are the real investigators holding up?" Clementine said, flicking her tiny head in the direction of a line of massive, grumpy bears clad in their dark blue uniforms seated at the counter and huddled over their plates.

Sheriff Samson and his cub-uties sat silently, picking at their salmon omelets. They hunched over their meals and coffee mugs, doing their best to ignore the growing grumbles of Chipper's diners. However, one customer was going to make that impossible.

"Whatcha gonna do about this, Samson?" Crank said, with an angry wing on his hip and a snarl in his voice. Crank was a crow who lived on the edge of the forest, and was generally dissatisfied with everything and everyone. His coal black feathers stood on end as he glared at Samson, waiting for a reply.

"About what?" Samson asked, feigning ignorance with a straight face.

"About this here robin'ry. I mean, robbery," Crank said. "This is what we pay you to do."

The other animals began to look up from their meals and turn their attention towards the pair, but Samson, as usual, remained placid and calm. This wasn't the first time that Crank had become worked up over something, and it surely wouldn't be the last.

Samson swiveled around on his stool to face Crank. The feisty, gruff crow stared up at the hulking bear sheriff and waited for a response.

Samson took a deep breath and said, "Tell you what,

Crank, me and the cub-uties are spending all day on this case, but we'd loooooooove to get your thoughts on it first."

Crank didn't catch the sarcasm in Samson's voice, and jumped right into his well-rehearsed investigative findings.

"I'm betting it was Rasso, that much should be obvious. That rat is always up to no good, and always mixed up in things like this; plus, Tumblecreek Road runs right through his old, dirty neighborhood. It'd be just like him to swipe a fancy Wind-O-Band-Go and turn it into some sort of nonsense. Heck, things like that were what got him in trouble when he worked as a garbage collector, remember?"

Some of the other customers grumbled in agreement.

"Crank," Samson began with a sigh, "we've already talked to Rasso, and he was on the other side of the forest the night the Wind-O-Band-Go went missing. Clarabelle and Claudette even backed up his story. They were with him."

The two waitresses turned red and scurried away.

"I'm just a-sayin', he's a rat, and he's always up to no good."

"We'll look into it, but thanks for your help as always, Crank," Samson said. He spun around on his seat and returned to his breakfast, although he had lost his appetite. Behind him, the accusations continued to grow louder as paws were pointed at one another and neighbor turned against neighbor.

Forest
Elm'enTree

CHAPTER TWELVE

It was a long night of school for Rocky and Wrigley. They were unable to focus. Their minds were busy, wondering how others were receiving their first issue of *While You Were Sleeping.*

At midnight meal, Rocky and Wrigley sat with Grover and Huck at a small round table in the corner of the cafeteria. Wrigley had held on to a couple of copies of the paper, and she was eager to share it with their friends.

"Best story I ever read," said Huck.

"Why, thank you," Wrigley said, beaming with pride. "Rocky and I had to hide under a disgusting dumpster all night in order to catch the thieves, but it was all worth it."

Huck shook his big green head. "Naw, Wrigley, naw. I mean don't git me wrong now, that there tale about the missing Windy-O-Bangy-O whatnot is great, but I was talkin' about that HopLympics story about ole Huck."

Wrigley's face turned red with an equal mix of embarrassment and anger.

Grover was silent as he read each story.

"So, what do you think, Grover?" Wrigley said through a smirk

The little goose scratched his beak with the edge of his wingtip. "I don't know," he said. "It's really good, but this cover story could be trouble."

"What do you mean, trouble?" Rocky asked, chomping through a pawful of redberries.

"I mean, it's kind of light on facts."

Wrigley's tiny teeth clenched in her mouth. "How dare you, Grover Gosling?" she said, working herself into a rage. "I'd like to see you do better."

"I didn't say I could do any better. It just seems like you think you maybe possibly saw some animals transporting the stolen Wind-O-Band-Go, but you really don't know who they were. Plus, you pin it on Rasso without being positive that you could identify him."

"Yeah, it do sound thatta way to me too," said Huck, his eyes wandering towards a courageous fly who was circling his head.

"I cannot believ—" Wrigley started, before falling silent with the rest of the cafeteria.

Every little eye turned towards the doorway, where Principal Ulysses T. Martin stood. The old 'possum had been in charge of Forest Elm'enTree for as long as anyone could remember. He had been the principal when Mom and Pop were students long ago; in the many years since, his legend had only grown.

He was lean and gray, stoic and calm. He also left little

doubt that he was in charge, even if he was generally pleasant. The students respected him, and truth be told, they all were a bit afraid of him

The school animals lowered their voices as the large 'possum walked slowly between their tables, each doing their best to avoid his stare.

Rocky, Wrigley, Grover and Huck kept their heads down and focused their attention on their thistleberry sandwiches and acorn berry bars. The silence of the usually noisy lunchroom hung heavily, until the large, slow-moving shadow of Principal Martin fell over Rocky and Wrigley's table and settled to a stop.

The 'possum gently laid a large hand on Rocky's shoulder, and quietly said, "Rocky. Wrigley. Could I have a word with both of you?"

The two Ringtail children looked at one another across the table, their eyes wide, their cheeks full of lunch.

Wrigley stammered, "Uh, sure. Yes, sir. Right now?"

The old 'possum nodded.

"What did we do?" Rocky asked.

"We can discuss it in my office," said the principal.

"Ooooos" and "Ummms" echoed around the lunchroom, but they were quickly silenced by the 'possum's icy stare.

Rocky and Wrigley gathered up what was left of their lunches and fell in behind Principal Martin. Their heads hung low as the procession slowly made its way towards the exit.

CHAPTER THIRTEEN

The Ringtails made their way down the school's empty hallways towards the principal's office, turning over in their heads the whys and the whats of how they could be in trouble.

Wrigley had never been to the principal's office before, at least not in this manner. She had been called in once before, to receive the news that she was at the top of her class. Principal Martin had been much more cheerful then…cheerful for him, at least.

Rocky, on the other paw, had been called in before for various minor infractions—like stashing snacks under his desk and tracking trash through the halls.

As they entered the office, the answer to their questions lay flat on Principal Martin's desk. There, spread amongst various papers and reports, was the first issue of *While You Were Sleeping.*

"Rocky, Wrigley, please have a seat."

The two children sat down in the hard wooden chairs that faced the principal's desk as he closed the door behind them.

Principal Martin eased into his own chair and folded his paws over the paper. "Rocky, Wrigley, your little paper has created quite the stir this morning."

The raccoons swallowed hard and tried to take deep breaths while they sat silently, considering what the problem might be.

"First, I will say that this forest has needed a newspaper for quite some time, and I am glad that you two took the initiative to see this to fruition." The principal looked down and began to fold the paper.

Rocky leaned close to his sister. "What's 'in-nitiative' mean?"

His sister cut her eyes toward him and grunted low in her throat.

"And what's 'fruit-ition' mean? Is that like a healthy snack?"

The principal answered for Wrigley. "It's means that I am impressed by your hard work and your ability to complete this project."

Rocky began to smile, but Wrigley knew there was a 'but' coming along very soon.

"But," the principal said, "your story about the theft is causing some problems. I was in Chipper's earlier this evening, and whoa, were there some upset folks."

"Why? What do you mean? What was going on at Chipper's?" Wrigley worriedly asked.

Principal Martin sighed. "You kids are in Chipper's

enough to know how these discussions go. Crank the Crow
was accusing Rasso. Terrence came out of the kitchen
to say it wasn't Rasso, and of course, Mockingbird Fred
backed him up. This only made Crank chirp more loudly
and accuse Terrence and his brother Virgil of being mixed
up in this mess. This infuriated cloudy-eyed Colonel
Cotton, whom I suppose thought he was back in the war.
Cotton was shouting at Crank, and Crank was shouting at
Terrence, and somewhere in all of this excitement, someone
shoved Dale Ribbit, who immediately fell over and grabbed
his good leg and claimed that he was suing Chipper. Finally,
Sheriff Samson had to break everyone up."

Wrigley began. "Principal Martin, we know that it might
be controversial and cause some problems, but we felt that
it was necessary to get this story out to the forest, so that
anyone with information pertaining to the crime could
contact the sheriff."

"I understand that, Wrigley, but by doing so, you
encouraged everyone in our community to blame everyone
else and to be suspicious of their neighbors."

The kids sat silently.

"There is no doubt that the Wind-O-Band-Go was stolen,
and there is no doubt that there are a few suspects. But did
you two really find any facts?"

"We saw some animals hauling it away from Gruffman's
Marsh."

"Right, and it was easy to infer from your story that you
think Rasso is behind it."

'What's "in-fur" m—"

"What I mean, Rocky, is that your story tries to pin the crime on someone without any real hard facts."

The kids looked down at their foot-paws in silence.

Wrigley reread the story in her head, as she had done so many times before, but now she could see a different perspective—a perspective that made the story unfair and harmful to others.

Finally, she spoke up. "He's right, Rocky. We messed up. We should have done a better job of reporting what we knew and what we were inferri—what we were guessing about and leading others to believe."

Rocky swallowed again and looked to the principal. "Does this mean we are in trouble?"

The principal leaned back in his chair. "No, you didn't break any school rules, and I don't think you intended to accuse anyone. You two have always been well-behaved raccoons," he glanced at Rocky, "even if you nose through the trash from time to time. You're both good students, and I know that your parents work really hard to provide for you."

At the mention of their parents, Wrigley began to tear up. She didn't want some mistake she and her brother had made let them down or embarrass them. She looked over at Rocky. His shoulders had sunk and his ears laid flat against his gray head.

"We should apologize," she said quietly. "It was our mistake, and we should try to make it right."

Principal Martin nodded slowly. "I think that would be the right thing to do, Wrigley."

Rocky looked up, with tears pooling in his big, black eyes. "If the entire forest is mad at us, how will we ever be able to apologize to everyone?"

Principal Martin picked up the paper and slid it across his desk towards the two Ringtail children. "Oh, you two are sharp kids. I'm sure you can figure out a way to make that happen," he said, with a kind, quick wink.

CHAPTER FOURTEEN

Rocky and Wrigley stared down at the dirt of the pawpath as they made their way towards the willow tree. Their first cover story had been an absolute disaster. They had mistaken guesses for facts, and even led their readers to believe that innocent animals, honest members of the forest, had been responsible for a crime. Their accusations had caused some real damage.

Inside the old tree, Pop Ringtail once again leafed through the pages of the newspaper. He was proud of his children for writing, designing, printing and distributing a newspaper for the forest—something that had been needed for a very long time. Plus, he couldn't help but smile as he thought about the tizzy the paper must have caused all of the nosey bluefeathers.

Pop looked up as Rocky and Wrigley came into the nightroom. The sky was just beginning to lighten, and the soft gossiping of the morning birds could be faintly heard in the neighboring trees.

"Have a seat," he said, folding the paper and tucking it beside his Laz-E-Log. Rocky and Wrigley squeezed onto the family's love branch. They were getting too big for it, and usually fought over who could sit there; today, neither protested, as they sat studying their tails, waiting for their punishment.

"Rough night?"

"Yes, sir," Wrigley said.

"I'm sure," Pop said, his voice firm but calm. "Your mother and I had to answer a lot of questions about you kids this morning. Critters wanted to know why you were accusing this animal or that animal of a crime. The fact that they each had their own opinion as to who was responsible would have been funny, had the crime not been so serious. They all wanted to know where you two had been eavesdropping, and I think they are all more than a little nervous about your second issue."

The kids squirmed in their seats.

"I'm sorry, Pop," Rocky said.

"Yeah," added Wrigley, "we didn't mean to accuse anyone of things they didn't do."

"I know you two didn't mean any harm, but you sure caused some. And I know you both thought you were helping out the forest by catching whoever swiped the Wind-O-Band-Go. Next time, though, be more careful; check and re-check your facts. My grandcoon, your great grandcoon, used to say 'wash twice and eat once.'"

Rocky looked up at the mention of eating, wrinkled his nose, and looked confused. "What does that mean?"

"What do we do before we eat something?"

"We dunk it in water," Wrigley answered, before Rocky

had the chance to respond.

"That's right, and why do we do that?"

Rocky was faster this time. "So that our food is softer, and it's cleaner. Sometimes I like to take several different kinds of berries, like blueberries and thistleberries and red berries, ooooo, red berries are my favorite, and squish 'em up and then wash 'em and eat them all at once. It's really good. But sometimes, I'll add just a little bit of—"

"Okay, Rocky. The point that I'm trying to make is that, in order to make sure our food is clean, we are extra careful to wash it twice and eat it once. Otherwise, we might get sick."

"Ohhhh, I get it," said Rocky.

"Just make sure that you 'wash twice and eat once' when it comes to publishing facts in your next issue."

Wrigley scoffed softly. "I doubt there'll be a next issue."

Rocky looked over at his sister and put his arm around her. She sat still and studied the cattail rug on which the love branch rested.

"That's for you and your brother to decide," Pop said softly.

"We really are sorry, Pop," Rocky said once again, tears beginning to well in his eyes.

"It'll be okay," he said. "Now, go wash your paws and get ready for bedtime gobble. Your mother will be home in just a bit."

Rocky and Wrigley pushed themselves off the love branch.

Pop waited until they were almost out of the nightroom before adding, "Oh, but before you do that, Sheriff Samson wanted to speak with you as well."

Rocky's stomach sank. Wrigley's eyes bulged.

"Sheriff Samson?" Rocky trembled.

"But why?" Wrigley asked.

"I don't know." Pop smiled, taking the tiniest bit of pleasure in his children's panic.

"Are we going to jail?" Rocky asked.

"I don't think so," Pop said, smiling, waiting for his kids to relax. "Buuuuuut…you might want to pack a bag, just in case," he said, with the tiniest of smiles.

CHAPTER FIFTEEN

Rocky and Wrigley stared upwards in awe as they approached the downwoods precinct station. The entrance sat inside the recess of two large gray stones, each with the etching of a barrel-chested former forest sheriff. Rocky read the inscriptions at the base of each statue as they slowly walked past.

"'Don't carry logs into the forest.' Sheriff Horace Hoot Owl," he read. "What in the world does that mean?"

Wrigley thought for a minute. "I suppose it means, don't drag a bunch of stuff with you if you are going to a place where those supplies are plentiful."

Rocky scratched his chin. "Hmmm," he said, "I guess that makes sense."

He tried the next one. "'Forest fortune—a ad-u-Vat.' What in the world? It says something about a forest too."

"It's Latin—a really old language," Wrigley said, standing in the doorway of the precinct, trying to hurry her brother along.

"Oh, okay," Rocky said. "What's it mean?"

"It means, 'Fortune favors the brave,'" Wrigley said.

Rocky looked at his sister and crinkled his face. "How do you know that? You don't speak Lat-In."

Wrigley rolled her eyes and pointed to the other side of the statue's base, where the inscription was translated into English.

They slowly walked into the dim cave filled with echoes and imposing walls. Large cub-uties sat behind desks, fumbling to type reports with thick, large paws.

Wrigley approached a particularly grumpy officer and said, "We are here to see Sheriff Samson. Can you please let him know we've arrived?"

The sleepy cub-uty looked up from his keyboard and peered through the reading glasses resting on the end of his large black snout at the tiny raccoon standing before him. He paused to regard her and the other coon, who was playing with his tail and staring at the ceiling, before grunting and nodding towards an office with an open door.

"Thank you for your help," Wrigley said.

The deputy grunted again and returned to his clumsy typing.

Rocky followed behind his sister and stopped her just short of Samson's door.

"Wrigley, I don't want to go in there. I'm scared."

Wrigley placed her hands on her brother's shoulders and did her best to smile. "It's okay, Rocky. It's going to be okay."

"But what if it's not? What if we go to jail?"

Wrigley hugged her little brother. "Rocky, we aren't going to go to jail. I promise. We are going to be okay."

Rocky sniffled, nodded his head, and once again followed behind his sister.

Samson's office was huge and intimidating. There were chairs of all shapes and sizes, and a small fireplace in a corner behind his desk. The sheriff was reading a report when Rocky and Wrigley tiptoed in.

Samson looked up from his desk. "Oh, hello," he said awkwardly. "Please, um, close the door behind you and have a seat." Samson had always struggled to talk to children. He tried his best, but he always seemed to say the wrong thing or to accidentally scare them in some way. He liked Rocky and Wrigley, and he tried his best to put them at ease.

Rocky looked at his sister with fear in his little black eyes. She did her best to camouflage her uncertainty as she nodded to say that it was okay to do as the sheriff had asked. Wrigley sat down in a chair that fit her best, while Rocky climbed into one that was more suited for a deer or a grizzly bear.

The sheriff chuckled. "Do you have enough room there, Rocky?"

The little raccoon nodded his head, doing his best not to cry.

Samson began. "I appreciate you kids coming down here. I'll get right to it, because it has been a long night for me, and I am sure it has been for you two as well. I just wanted to let you know that we caught the culprit…or, should I say, culprits."

Samson paused as the two raccoons looked at one another with wide eyes. "Would you like to hear about it?"

Rocky and Wrigley nodded eagerly.

"Okay," Samson said, "earlier this evening, my cub-uties and I received a tip about a strange new luxury nest that was precariously perched in a high-rise branch overlooking Goodnight Road."

Rocky and Wrigley's ears perked up.

"Upon arriving at the scene, we observed a particularly chatty blue jay in the process of hurriedly filling the item with branches, twigs, and leaves, in an apparent attempt to hide all identifying markings on the item and its contents. I questioned the branch's occupant, a Miss Maybelle, and it didn't take long to get the full story from her."

The kids stared with their mouths hanging open. *Maybelle?!? The gossipy blue jay?!? Their neighbor?!? The whole reason they'd started the paper in the first place?!?!*

"Maybelle stole the Wind-O-Band-Go?" Rocky gasped.

"Not exactly," Samson said, holding up a large paw, trying to hold Rocky back from jumping to another conclusion. "Maybelle is a, well, how do I say this nicely—"

"A gossip?" Rocky blurted.

Wrigley swatted at him.

Samson chuckled. "Perhaps. But what I was going to say is that Maybelle is old-ish, and she alone could not swipe a heavy Wind-O-Band-Go."

"She got someone to do it for her, and they were the ones we saw that night on Tumblecreek Road," Wrigley pieced together.

"That's right. Because of your reporting, which we'll get to in a moment, we were able to gather several peculiar footprints from the mud on Tumblecreek Road. Owl tracks. Two sets, in fact."

"The Hoot Owls?" Wrigley asked.

"Two of The Hoot Owls—Moonie and 'Squito. It seems Maybelle paid them to swipe the Wind-O-Band-Go, so that she could turn it into a new high-rise luxury pent-nest. Apparently her current nest is old and falling apart."

"It wasn't Rasso?"

"Nope. Not this time, at least," Samson said, looking up from his notes.

The kids sat in stunned silence as their minds worked through the details— *Maybelle's frequent trips to ask for Pop's help with repairs, her chatty nature, her need to keep up appearances.*

"I questioned Chirp and Angus, and they were unaware that this took place, but we arrested Moonie, 'Squito, and Miss Maybelle about an hour ago. They are currently awaiting their hearing before Judge Foxx."

Samson closed the file folder on his desk and looked down at the Ringtail children.

"That should just about cover the crime…now, let's talk about your paper."

Rocky and Wrigley's heads dropped as they sunk back into their chairs.

"I know that you two did not mean any harm, but you sure caused a stir amongst the forest community. We got calls and visits from all sorts of critters—animals who've never had a clever thought in their lives were coming up with all sorts of wild theories. It's made my cub-uties grumpier than usual," Samson said with a short laugh. "And after that episode at Chipper's this morning, ole Crank will have nothing but gray feathers left."

"We are really sorry, Sheriff Samson."

"I know you are, Wrigley. And I know that you both thought you were helping out. I appreciate the effort. But you need to be a bit more diligent in your reporting, and maybe write an apology to your readers."

Rocky thought back over all of the mistakes they had made and all the trouble they had caused—trouble for one animal in particular.

He looked at Wrigley. "What about Rasso?"

She hung her head and thought about the rat they barely knew but had accused.

Samson sat silently reflecting for a moment as well. Rasso had been a thorn in his side for years, and it was true that he was typically behind the minor crimes in the forest. Even so, Rasso didn't deserve to be accused of something he had not done.

"I'll leave it to you to decide if and how you'd like to apologize to Rasso specifically," he said softly.

"We can do that," Wrigley said, discreetly wiping her eyes.

"Will we be able to work on that while we're in jail?" Rocky asked.

Samson laughed so loudly that it startled the little raccoons.

"Oh, I'm sorry. I didn't mean to scare you. Rocky, you two are not going to jail. This was a simple, honest mistake, and you didn't commit a crime."

"Oh, pssshew," Rocky said, wiping his brow, "that's a relief."

"If you apologize and work to make this right, I think you can avoid jail time," Samson said with a smile. "Okay, you kids can go."

The Ringtails got up to leave, and Samson repeated, "Just be sure to double check your facts before you write anything else."

"Right. We should wash twice and eat once," said Rocky.

Samson gave them a confused looked. "Huh?"

"Oh, just ignore him," Wrigley said, as she hurried her brother out the door.

CHAPTER SIXTEEN

Once again, Rocky and Wrigley spent a long night copying issue after issue of their paper; however, this time, the lone article was much shorter:

To All of Our Forest Readers:

The publishers of *While You Were Sleeping* would like to sincerely apologize for our recent article detailing a local theft. In our haste to report the incident, we did not verify certain facts. Our errors in judgment and reporting led to false accusations toward our forest friends. We regret these mistakes and will seek to avoid them in the future.

We would also like to offer a special apology to Rasso. In our haste to publish our report, we accused him of a crime he didn't commit; it was unwarranted, and for that, we are especially sorry.

This will be the final issue of our newspaper, and we have no plans to publish in the future. We appreciate your support over the course of this very short run, and we hope that you will accept our apology.

Sincerely,

Rocky and Wrigley Ringtail

After each issue was copied, the raccoons dipped their front paws into a pad of red clay and pressed them at the bottom of each page, the way all raccoons sign their names. They then walked to the washbasin and scrubbed their paws clean.

"I'm sad, Wrigley," said Rocky, his head bowed and his eyes looking into the water. "I was really having fun being an in-vest-i-ga-tive journalist."

"I know," his sister said. "I'm sad too, but we're doing the right thing."

"Do you think everyone will still be mad at us?"

"I don't know, Rocky. I don't know."

Slivers of sunlight had just begun to ease through the long, thin branches of Ringtail Willow, casting its golden warmth into the trunk of the old tree.

Mom peeked around the door of her children's bedroom, watching Rocky and Wrigley bundling up copies of the paper.

"Did you finish up?" she asked, her voice tender as she put an arm around each of them.

"Yes, ma'am," Rocky said. "We are going to go drop these off, and then come right home."

Mom looked down at her two tired babies. "Tell you what—why don't we get up a bit early, and Pop and I will help you. We'll do it together. How does that sound?"

Wrigley and Rocky nodded their heads.

"Good. I know you two are worn out, so why don't you

go ahead and get ready for bed," Mom said, giving Rocky and Wrigley another quick hug before turning to leave the room.

"Mom," Rocky asked, as she stopped in the doorway, "can Wrigley and I sleep with you and Pop this morning?"

Mom smiled sweetly. "Of course you can."

EPILOGUE

The day was beginning for some, and the night ending for others, and for the Ringtails, it was time for them to get still inside the comfort of their cozy tree. The next night would bring more adventures, but for now, those stories would have to wait.

Even though the case of the missing Wind-O-Band-Go had been solved, Chirp and the Hoot Owls were no more, and Miss Maybelle would soon have a bevy of brand new sordid tales following her very brief stint in the local forest jail. Maybe one day Rocky and Wrigley would publish another issue of *While You Were Sleeping*, but for now, that decision could wait. The Ringtail children had learned a valuable lesson—one that they would not soon forget.

As the morning sunlight began to fill their little home, Pop drew the curtains of the nightroom, and the sleepy raccoon family curled their ringed tails around one another and drifted off to sleep.

THE END